The Little Things

Emma Dodd

templar books
an imprint of Candlewick Press

It's the little things that matter.
It's the little things that count.
It's not the biggest or the best
or the largest amount.

It's kisses in the morning
when we wake up with the dawn,
getting ready for a new day
with a stretch and a yawn.

It's spending time together.
It's watching clouds float by.

It's saying "sorry" when we're wrong . . .

and "good job" when we try.

It's smiling at a stranger.

It's giving friends a hug.

It's cuddling up out of the rain,
warm and dry and snug.

It's helping one another.
It's trying to be kind.

It's waiting for a buddy
if one gets left behind.

It's playing and it's talking.
It's laughter and it's fun.
It's heading home together
when the day is done.

It's all these little things

that make you such a special you.

And it's the very **big** reason
why I love you like I do.

First US edition 2021
First UK edition published by Templar Books,
an imprint of Bonnier Books UK, 2022

Library of Congress Catalog Card Number pending
ISBN 978-1-5362-2001-8

21 22 23 24 25 26 LEO 10 9 8 7 6 5 4 3 2 1

Printed in Heshan, Guangdong, China

This book was typeset in Eureka Sans.
The illustrations were created digitally.

TEMPLAR BOOKS
an imprint of
Candlewick Press
99 Dover Street
Somerville, Massachusetts 02144

www.candlewick.com